All children have a great ambition to read to themselves...

and a sense of achievement when they can do so. The **read it yourself** series has been devised to satisfy their ambition. Since many children learn from the Ladybird Key Words Reading Scheme, these stories have been based to a large extent on the Key Words List, and the tales chosen are those with which children are likely to be familiar.

The series can of course be used as supplementary reading for any reading scheme.

Heidi is intended for children reading up to Book 5c of the Ladybird Reading Scheme. The following words are additional to the vocabulary used at that level —

Heidi, mother, father, Aunt, Dete, day, mountains, went, way, grandfather, friend, live, old, goats, sleep, hay, loft, back, next, pasture, stay, every, happy, winter, grandmother, did, could, daughter, sick, don't, miss, Clara, servant, teach, manners, been, long, waited, night, dreamt, noises, white, ghost, wrote, doctor, were, wonderful, carrying, jealous, push, tried, feet, worried, sorry, horrible

A list of other titles at the same level will be found on the back cover.

Published by Ladybird Books Ltd Loughborough Leicestershire UK
Ladybird Books Inc Lewiston Maine 04240 USA

Heidi

adapted by Fran Hunia
from the original story by Johanna Spyri

illustrated by Lynne Willey

Ladybird Books

Heidi was a little girl who had no mother or father. She was looked after by her Aunt Dete.

One day Aunt Dete said, "Come on, Heidi. We are going up the mountain."

They put all Heidi's things in a bag and off they went.

They walked and walked. On the way a friend of Aunt Dete's stopped them.

"Where are you taking the little girl, Dete?" she asked.

"I am taking her to see her grandfather," said Aunt Dete. "Heidi is going to live with him."

"What!" said Dete's friend. "He is an old man. He will not want to look after a little girl!"

"He has to," said Aunt Dete. "I am going to work in Frankfurt."

Heidi and Aunt Dete walked on.
They saw a boy who was taking
some goats up the mountain. It
was Peter. Heidi walked on with
him to the house where her
grandfather lived. Grandfather
came out to see who was there.

Aunt Dete said, "This is Heidi. She is going to live with you from now on," and with that Dete ran off down the mountain.

Peter went to get Grandfather's goats from the goat house, then he went on his way.

Heidi looked about her.

"Please take me in to see the house, Grandfather," she said.

They went in.

"Now, where can I sleep?" asked Heidi. She went up into the hay loft. "I like it up here," she said. "Can I make my bed in the hay?"

Grandfather helped Heidi to make her bed in the hay. Then they went down again to eat.

That afternoon Peter came back with the goats. Grandfather milked one of the goats.

"Here you are, Heidi," he said.

"Here is some goat's milk for you."

Heidi had her milk, and then she went to sleep in her bed up in the hay loft.

The next day Peter came again.

"Where are you going with the goats?" asked Heidi.

"I am taking them up to the pasture," said Peter. "Do you want to come with me?"

"Yes, please," said Heidi. "Can I go, Grandfather?"

"Yes," said Grandfather. "Off you go."

Heidi and Peter went up the mountain with the goats.

Heidi liked it up on the pasture. She liked the trees and the flowers, and she had fun playing with Peter and the goats.

Every day after that Heidi went up to the pasture with Peter and the goats. She was so happy.

Then winter came. The goats had to stay in the goat house all day, and Peter had to go to school.

Some afternoons he came to see Heidi and her grandfather. One day he asked Heidi to go and see his grandmother, who lived a little way down the mountain.

Heidi wanted to go back then with Peter, but Grandfather said, "No, Heidi, not now. I will take you to see her one day soon."

One day Grandfather said,
"Come on, Heidi. Now I will take
you to see Peter's grandmother."

They went down the mountain
to Peter's house, but Heidi's
grandfather did not go in. He went
home again. Heidi went into the
house.

"Who is it?" asked the grandmother, who could not see.

"It is me, Heidi. I have come to see you."

Peter's grandmother was pleased to have a friend to talk to. They talked all afternoon. Then Heidi said, "I must go now, Grandmother. I will come and see you again soon."

One day Aunt Dete came to see
Heidi's grandfather. "I have come
to get Heidi," she said. "I want to
take her to Frankfurt with me. I
know of a man who has a sick
daughter. He is looking for a friend
to live with her. I am going to take
Heidi there."

"Go away," said the
grandfather. "Heidi is happy here."

"But she is a big girl now," said
Dete. "She must go to school.
Come on, Heidi."

"No!" said Heidi. "I like living here with Grandfather. I don't want to go away."

"Come on, Heidi," said Aunt Dete. "Grandfather will be pleased to see you go, and you will like Frankfurt."

"Can I come back home if I want to?" asked Heidi.

"Yes, yes," said Aunt Dete. "Now come on, or we will miss the train."

Heidi and her aunt went to the house where the sick girl, Clara lived. Then Aunt Dete went off and Heidi stayed there with Clara and the servants.

Clara could not walk. She had to sit in her chair all day. She was pleased to have a friend to talk to, but the servant who looked after Clara did not like Heidi.

"I will have to teach you some manners," she said.

The servant talked on and on, but it had been a long day for Heidi. She went to sleep in her chair!

Next day Heidi looked out of the window. There were no trees or flowers. All she could see were streets and shops and houses.

"I don't like it here," said Heidi. "I must go home soon."

Then Clara's teacher came and the two girls had to do some school work.

That afternoon Heidi talked to Clara about her home on the mountain, about Grandfather, Peter, and Grandmother. Clara liked having a friend to talk to.

One day Clara's grandmother came to stay. She liked Heidi and was kind to her. Heidi liked Clara and her grandmother, but she was not happy in Frankfurt. She missed her grandfather, and Peter and his grandmother. Every night she dreamt that she was at home in the mountains.

One day the servants said that there had been noises in the night. The next night one of the servants saw a white thing.

"It must be a ghost," they all said. They wrote to Clara's father, who was away. "You must come home," they said. "There is a ghost in the house."

Clara's father came home and
asked his friend the doctor to sit up
with him at night and wait for the
ghost. They talked as they waited.
Then there was a noise. They
looked out and saw a white thing.
It was Heidi!

"So this is our ghost!" they said.
"What are you doing here?"

"I don't know," said Heidi.

"Come on, Heidi," said the doctor.
"I will take you back to bed."

The doctor put Heidi back into bed. "What were you dreaming about?" he asked kindly.

"Every night I dream that I am at home in the mountains. I dream of Grandfather, and Peter and his grandmother," said Heidi.

"I see," said the doctor. "And were you happy in the mountains?"

"Yes," said Heidi.

"You are not happy here, are you?" said the doctor.

"I must not say that," said Heidi. "They are so kind to me here."

"I see," said the doctor. "Now go to sleep and I will see what I can do to help you."

The doctor went down to talk to Clara's father. "Heidi has been walking in her sleep," he said. "She is a sick little girl. She must go home."

Heidi was pleased to be going home, but Clara wanted her to stay.

"She has to go," said Clara's father. "But you can go and see her one day. Now come on, Heidi, or you will miss the train."

One of the servants went on the train with Heidi, then he went home and Heidi walked up the mountain. She came to Peter's house and went in to have a little talk to his grandmother. Then she went on.

Heidi went into her grandfather's house. Grandfather looked up. "Heidi!" he said. "How wonderful to have you back!"

"It is good to be home," said Heidi. "They were kind to me in Frankfurt, but I missed you, Grandfather."

Soon Peter came down the mountain with the goats. He was pleased to see Heidi too. They talked and talked. Then Peter had to go home.

Heidi had some goat's milk, then she went up to the hay loft. Grandfather had taken her bed away, but they soon put it back again. Heidi did not walk in her sleep that night. She was so happy to be home.

Every day Heidi went up the
mountain with Peter and the goats.
Then one day Clara wrote to say
that she and her grandmother were
coming to see Heidi.

For two days Heidi did not go up
the mountain with Peter. She
stayed at home and waited for her
friends to come.

Heidi waited and waited. Then
she saw some men carrying Clara
up the mountain in a chair.
Grandmother was there too. Heidi
was so pleased to see them! They
all talked and talked. Then
Grandfather said, "Do you want to
stay here with us, Clara?"

"Yes, please," said Clara. "Can I stay, Grandmother?"

"Yes," said her grandmother. "It will be good for you to stay up here in the mountains. I will come back and get you when winter is coming."

That night the two girls went to sleep up in the hay loft. They were so happy.

The next day Peter came to get the goats. "Come on, Heidi," he said.

"I am not going up to the pasture," said Heidi. "I have a friend here."

Peter went off with the goats, but he was jealous. He missed Heidi.

Heidi said to her grandfather, "Can Clara go up to the pasture one day, Grandfather?"

"Yes," said Grandfather. "I will push her up in her chair."

The next day Peter came to get
the goats. He saw Clara's chair by
the house. He was so jealous that
he pushed it down the mountain
and ran off!

Soon Heidi came out to get the chair. It was not there! Heidi and her grandfather looked and looked for it, but they had to give up.

"I will have to carry you up the mountain, Clara," said Grandfather.

He carried Clara up to the pasture and then he went down to look for her chair.

Clara and Heidi had a happy day up on the pasture. Then Heidi said, "I must go and look at the flowers. Wait here with Peter and the goats, Clara. I will be back soon."

Heidi went to look at the flowers. "I do want Clara to see them," she said. She went back to Clara and Peter.

"Come on, Peter," she said. "You must help me. I want to take Clara to see the flowers."

Peter and Heidi tried to carry Clara, but they could not do it. Clara tried to help by putting her

feet down. Then she said, "Look!
I can walk!"

Heidi and Peter saw her walk to
the flowers.

That afternoon Grandfather
came to get Clara. "Clara can walk!"
said Heidi and Peter. Clara walked a
little way for Grandfather to see.

Every day after that Clara
walked a little more. Then she and
Heidi wrote to Grandmother and
asked her to come. They did not

say that Clara could walk.

Soon Grandmother came. She saw that Clara was not in her chair. "What is going on?" she asked. Then Clara walked to her grandmother.

"This is wonderful!" said Grandmother.

Clara and Heidi saw a man coming up the mountain. "It's Daddy!" said Clara.

Clara's father looked at his daughter. "Can this be my little Clara?" he asked.

"Yes, Daddy," said Clara. "Look!"

Clara walked to her father.

"You can walk!" he said. "How wonderful!"

Peter came down the mountain with the goats. He was worried.

"What is that boy so worried about?" asked Clara's grandmother.

"I know," said Grandfather. "Was it you who pushed Clara's chair down the mountain, Peter?"

"Yes," said Peter. "I'm sorry. It was a horrible thing to do."

"Yes, it was," said Grandmother. "But some good has come of it. Clara can walk now, and we have to thank you for that. Now come on, Peter. We want to see your grandmother. Will you take us?"

"Yes," said Peter. "She will be pleased to have you."

And she was.